dogs have cute little puppies.

tortoises lay eggs and bury them in the dirt.

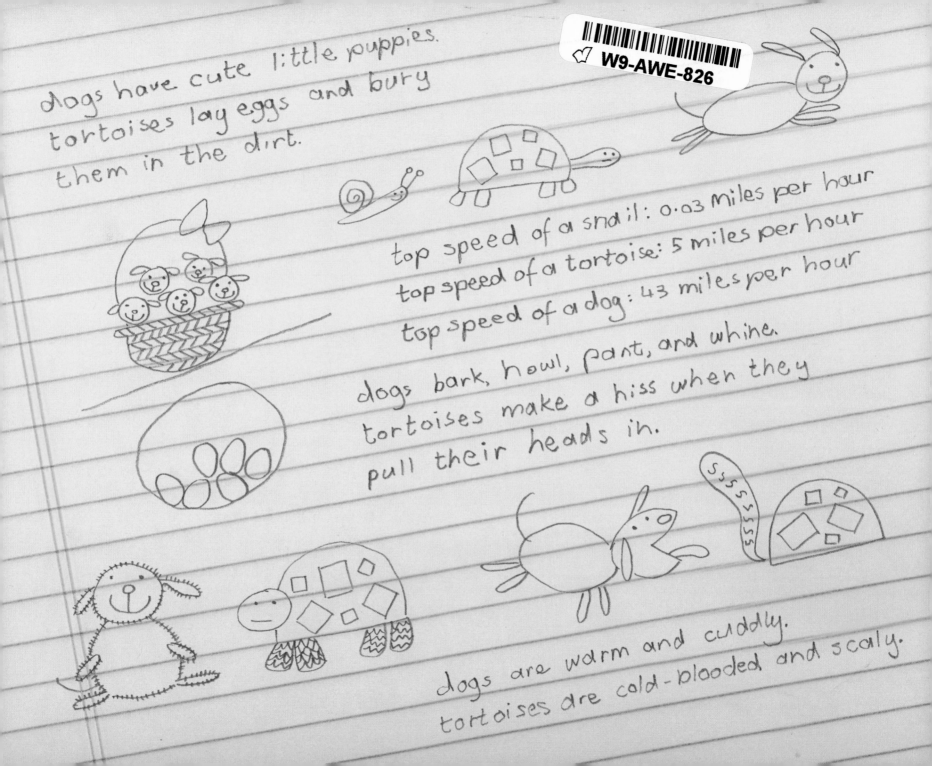

top speed of a snail: 0.03 miles per hour

top speed of a tortoise: 5 miles per hour

top speed of a dog: 43 miles per hour

dogs bark, howl, pant, and whine.

tortoises make a hiss when they pull their heads in.

dogs are warm and cuddly.

tortoises are cold-blooded and scaly.

Who Wants a TORTOISE?

BY
DAVE KEANE

ILLUSTRATED BY
K.G. CAMPBELL

Alfred A. Knopf New York

I've been waiting my whole life to get a puppy,
a rascally guy with a waggly tail.

I make lists of cute dog names.

I read about training puppies.

I dream of all the adventures I'll have
with my trusty dog at my side.

A puppy is the ONLY thing I want
for my birthday.

But the present
with the holes in the top . . .   . . . doesn't have a puppy in it.

"What is that?" whispers Sasha. She has a golden retriever.
"Is it dead?" asks Emily. She has a dalmatian.
"It's a tortoise," says Eric, who's an expert on gross stuff.
"That's a reptile. It has cold blood." He has a wiener dog.

"A tortoise?" I croak.
"WHO WANTS A TORTOISE?!"

I don't cry . . . until I open Sasha's present.

After everyone leaves, Daddy says he's told me a million times that he's allergic to dogs.

"Did you ever think I might be allergic to a dumb tortoise?" I shout.

You never get time-outs because of a dog.

I don't have a list of cute tortoise names,
so I don't name him anything.

"Hey, you, tortoise."
He doesn't seem to mind, but it's impossible
to tell what a tortoise is thinking.

I decide to see what my
new lump of a pet can do.

"Fetch, boy, fetch!"

Turns out tortoises won't fetch anything.

They also do NOT like rolling over. But when it comes to playing dead, my tortoise is an expert.

"Gimme a kiss!"

Unlike dogs, tortoises will not lick your face.

At least a tortoise doesn't squirm when you play makeover. I do his nails with Sparkling Raspberry Delight.

"But he looks like a princess!"

"You shouldn't use a glue stick on such a majestic creature."

Mommy and I both make our mad faces for the rest of the day. I think my tortoise is mad too, but it's still impossible to tell what he's thinking.

Grammy and Grandpa come for a visit and bring me a birthday present: a tortoise book.

"Tortoises have been around since the dinosaurs."

"Whoa, that's even older than you."

My book says a tortoise like mine was the first reptile to go into space. So I make my tortoise a space suit. He actually looks kind of brave.

If a tortoise can fly into space, going for a walk
should be easy. But there's no place for the
leash. Nothing a little duct tape can't fix.

It turns out tortoises are actually pretty good at some things.
When Sasha and I have a lemonade stand, we also sell
chances to hold a real-life tortoise.

We sell more tortoise than lemonade.

Eric and I set up a racetrack. My guy wins by a mile.

On sharing day at school, my tortoise poops
on Brendan's desk, which is totally great.

"Dumb turtle," he says.
"How dare you," I say.
"Tortoises hate being called turtles.
Besides, everyone knows turtles live
in water and tortoises live on land."
"They do?" he says.

I discover there's one thing tortoises are *too* good at: hide-and-seek.

After twenty minutes, we start to panic.

"HERE, TORTOISE, TORTOISE, TORTOISE!" we shout a billion times, but a tortoise almost never comes when you call.

We knock on everyone's door.

We hang fifty signs and offer our lemonade money for a reward.

When it gets dark, I set out a plate of butter lettuce, which is like chocolate chip cookies to a tortoise. And I leave the porch light on, just in case.

Days go by.
I put fresh butter lettuce out every night.

I can't sleep with my poor little tortoise out in the big world all by himself, with only his shell to protect him. He never made any noise, but the house seems quieter without him.

A week later, Mommy happens to mention that Mrs. Gilbert down the street thinks a rabbit is nibbling her turnips and cabbages.

I'm out the door so fast I forget to swallow my spaghetti.

"YOU NAUGHTY LITTLE TORTOISE!" I shout.

"Don't worry," I tell Mrs. Gilbert.
"This rascally guy with the waggly tail belongs to me!"

Somebody is extra shy about all the attention at his welcome-home parade.

We celebrate by painting our toenails
Sparkling Raspberry Delight.

That night, after we settle down in our beds, the whole
house feels quiet, but this time it's a tortoise kind of quiet.

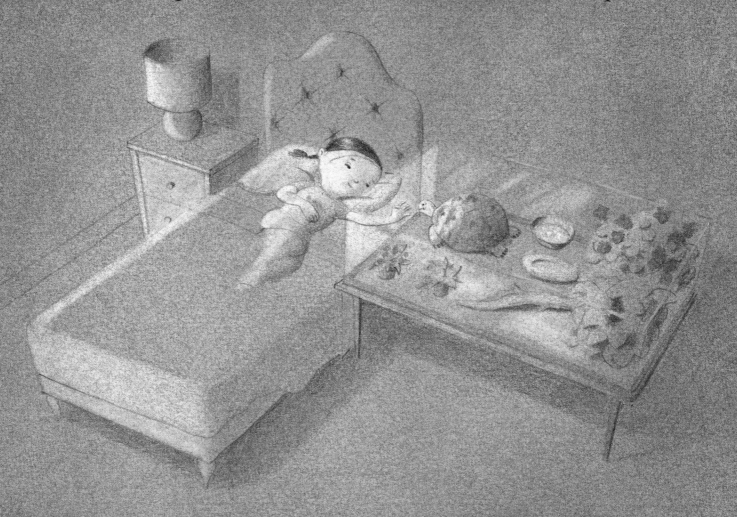

Just before I fall asleep, I remember my favorite
name on my list of cute dog names. It's perfect.
"Good night, Rover," I say into the darkness.

Then I dream of all the adventures I'll
have with my trusty tortoise at my side.

For my pet tortoise, Shelly,
who taught me you can never tell
what a tortoise is thinking
—D.K.

To Felix and Alice, with love
—K.G.C.

THIS IS A BORZOI BOOK PUBLISHED BY ALFRED A. KNOPF
Text copyright © 2016 by Dave Keane
Jacket art and interior illustrations copyright © 2016 by K.G. Campbell
All rights reserved. Published in the United States by Alfred A. Knopf,
an imprint of Random House Children's Books,
a division of Penguin Random House LLC, New York.
Knopf, Borzoi Books, and the colophon are registered trademarks of Penguin Random House LLC.

Visit us on the Web! randomhousekids.com
Educators and librarians, for a variety of teaching tools, visit us at RHTeachersLibrarians.com

Library of Congress Cataloging-in-Publication Data
Keane, David.
Who wants a tortoise? / by Dave Keane ; illustrated by K.G. Campbell. — First edition.
pages cm.
Summary: Expecting a dog for her birthday, a girl is upset and furious when she gets a tortoise instead,
but soon learns that even a tortoise can be a good pet.
ISBN 978-0-385-75417-0 (trade) — ISBN 978-0-385-75418-7 (lib. bdg.) — ISBN 978-0-385-75419-4 (ebook)
1. Testudinidae—Juvenile fiction. 2. Pets—Juvenile fiction. 3. Birthdays—Juvenile fiction. [1. Turtles—Fiction.
2. Pets—Fiction.] I. Campbell, K. G. (Keith Gordon), illustrator. II. Title.
PZ7.K2172Wh 2015   [E]—dc23   2015007166

The illustrations in this book were created using watercolor and colored pencil on watercolor paper.

MANUFACTURED IN CHINA
July 2016   10 9 8 7 6 5 4 3 2   First Edition

tortoises? terrific!

friends for life, many tortoises
live for 100 years. some have
lived for more than 150 years.

a tortoise shell is made of
keratin, like horse hooves
and our fingernails.

some tortoises can go a year
or more without drinking water.
they can get their water
from food.